OWJC

D0612694

A SNOW DAY FOR
PLUM!

MATT PHELAN

A SNOW DAY FOR
PLUM!

📖 Greenwillow Books
An Imprint of HarperCollins*Publishers*

A Snow Day for Plum!
Copyright © 2023 by Matt Phelan

The text of this book is set in Charlotte Book.
Book design by Sylvie Le Floc'h

Library of Congress Control Number: 2022950006
ISBN 9780063079205 (hardcover)

22 23 24 25 26 LBC 5 4 3 2 1
First Edition
Greenwillow Books

For my mom

BRING THE ZOO* TO YOU!
* NOT THE ENTIRE ZOO (SORRY).
MEET A REAL ZOO-KEEPER!
PET A FRIENDLY ANIMAL!
CALL FOR DETAILS!

Chapter One
The Traveling Athensville Zoo

Plum the peacock sat still and quiet. He was usually pretty peppy. His friends at the Athensville Zoo would say he was cheerful and chatty. But this morning, Plum did not feel like his usual peppy, cheerful, chatty self. Plum felt a little bit—just a little bit—scared.

"Isn't this exciting?" asked Meg.

Plum and Meg sat in individual peacock cages. Next to them were cages that contained Kevin, a giant elephant shrew (not giant, nor an elephant); Jeremy, a former street cat, now happily owned by Lizzie the zookeeper; Myrna, a colorful parrot; and Itch, a ningbing (small mammal, unusual in many ways).

"'Exciting' is too mild a word," said Itch. "'Thrilling,' perhaps. Is there a word that aptly describes the sensation of fulfilling one's destiny?"

"Nausea?" asked Kevin, who was feeling a little wobbly in the belly.

You see, these fine animals of the Athensville

Zoo were not, in fact, at the zoo. They were bouncing along in the back of a zoo van. They were on their way to visit Romeburg Elementary School.

"Just think," said Itch, "in less than an hour, I shall be lecturing eager young minds about the great wonders of the animal kingdom!"

"I think Lizzie is actually doing the lecturing part," said Meg.

"Perhaps—dare I dream?—I will use the SMART Board!" said Itch, ignoring Meg.

"Maybe the visit will be canceled," said Plum in a small voice.

"Canceled?" said Itch. "Why on earth would it be canceled?"

"Well," said Plum a bit louder, "I think the school might soon be buried in snow."

The others followed Plum's gaze out the van's back windows. The sky was heavy and gray, and large snowflakes were falling.

"Pshaw!" said Itch. "It is nothing but a flurry."

"Squawk," said Myrna, who never used actual words of any kind, animal or human.

Lizzie the zookeeper, who was driving the van, tuned the radio to a news station. An announcer's voice came through the static.

" . . . the sudden snowstorm has taken us all by surprise. Well, that's weather nowadays for you! Snow accumulation could be . . . let's see what this note says . . . intense? No. Immense, I think. Anyway, it looks like we're getting a lot of snow today. Stay put and stay safe!"

Lizzie turned the radio off.

"Hoo boy, friends," said Lizzie. "This day may not go as planned."

The plan had been to visit kindergarten through fifth grade. Lizzie would talk about the zoo and the animals, and the children would be allowed to pet the animals and ask questions.

In Plum's opinion, this plan had (at minimum) the following three problems:

1) What if the schoolchildren didn't like him?

2) What if he got lost?

3) What if he made a mistake?

Plum never worried about any of that back at the zoo. There he proudly served with his fellow peacocks as a free-range ambassador to all zoo visitors. He mingled. He guided. He delighted. At the Athensville Zoo, Plum *always* knew what to do.

"I think our presentation may be canceled today," said Lizzie.

Itch made a sort of strangled noise.

"Oh, no," said Meg. "Won't that be terribly disappointing, Plum?"

Plum did not feel disappointed at all. In fact, he was beginning to feel a little bit—just a little bit—peppy.

Chapter Two
24-Hour Gym Class

"I guess you better turn this old van around and head back to the zoo, Lizzie," said Plum.

Lizzie, being human, could not actually understand animal language. She did not respond to Plum. She was having a difficult time seeing the road in the increasingly heavy snow.

The van skidded once. It skidded again. Quite

a lot of snow had fallen in the past few minutes.

"There's the school!" said Lizzie. "We'll find out what the situation is. I don't think it's safe to drive back in this storm."

No school visit? No way home? What would they do?

The van trudged into the parking lot. Lizzie hopped from the van and sunk into several inches of snow. A man in earmuffs waved from the front door.

"Hello! Ms. Rodriquez?" called the man over the squall.

"Call me Lizzie," said Lizzie, making her way against the wind to join him.

"I'm Principal Franklin. I'm afraid we must cancel today's visit."

"Yes, I thought you might," said Lizzie.

"The children have all been sent home. The news says we might get three feet of snow! Oh, my. And tomorrow is Saturday, so we will need to completely reschedule."

"Spring might be good," suggested Lizzie through chattering teeth.

"Indeed," agreed the principal. "However, we can't have you driving back in this blizzard."

"Where can we all stay?"

"The animals will be perfectly safe here at the school for the night. We have a secure area in the gym all set for them. They will be quite comfortable."

"Great! Thank you," said Lizzie.

"And for you, Lizzie, we have a treat! I have booked you a room at Doily Gables, Romeburg's finest inn!"

"That's very kind of you."

"Our pleasure. We have a special relationship with Doily Gables. Every room in the school has a free calendar they give out each year! We get the calendars because our visiting authors stay exclusively at Doily Gables. We've hosted Jeanne Birdsall, James Howe, Jennifer Holm, Jerry Pinkney . . . have you ever noticed how many authors have *J* names?"

"I've never thought about it."

"Hmm," said Principal Franklin. "Jeff Mack, Jane Yolen, Jarrett Kro . . . Kro . . . "

"Krosoczka," said Lizzie. "I don't mean to interrupt, but perhaps we should get the animals inside."

"Yes, absolutely!" said the principal. "Let me get the doors."

Inside the van, the animals remained quiet. Except for Itch.

"Are you sobbing, Itch?" asked Kevin.

"No, Kevin," said Itch. "My eyes are just

watery from all of this whiteness. It's called snow blindness, for your information."

"We're not going home?" asked Plum.

"Looks like we're going to have an adventure, Plum," said Jeremy.

"A sleepover!" said Meg. "This will be fun!"

"Yeah," said Plum quietly. "Loads of fun."

Lizzie opened the van doors.

"Change of plans, my friends! You are all now temporarily enrolled at Romeburg Elementary School!"

Lizzie had apologized repeatedly to the animals about the need to spend the night in their traveling cages. The cages were large, comfortable, and filled with food and water . . . but they were still cages. It was for their own safety, Lizzie had said.

Even Jeremy the cat was in his cage since Doily Gables did not allow any pets, especially cats. The inn already had twelve cats, and they were "too precious and special" to mingle with outsiders.

The gymnasium was big, with high windows. The animals could see the snow continue to fall. The school was dark and empty. The only sound was a gentle chirp from Myrna. Most of the animals were glum, but one seemed very cheerful about their safe, snug confinement.

"Could be worse!" piped Plum. "We can tell stories or sing songs. Who knows a knock-knock joke?"

"Knock, knock," said Itch.

"Who's there?" asked Plum.

"You. Unfortunately," said Itch. "If we are to be imprisoned and robbed of our chance for glory and the thrill of lecturing, I must insist that you all remain silent and miserable."

"I think Plum is right," said Meg. "We should at least try to make the best of it."

"It's good that we're all together," said Kevin. "I'd hate it if they'd split us up."

Jeremy stretched a paw through the bars of his cage.

"I might be able to pick this lock," said Jeremy. "Then we could at least explore the school. . . . " He extended a claw but couldn't quite reach.

"Hey, Myrna," said Jeremy. "You have a good curved beak. Can you pick the lock?"

"Chirrup!" said Myrna. She didn't move.

"Do you think Myrna understands our talking but doesn't talk herself, or is it all just noise to her?" asked Kevin.

"Choop! Choop!" said Myrna.

"Some birds of her species are capable of talk,"
said Itch. "Some are simply . . . colorful."

"Beep!" said Myrna.

"Hopeless," said Itch.

They all fell silent again.

"What are you still doing in there?"

Three white mice stood in front of the cages.

"It's a *snow* day," said one mouse.

"Yeah," said another. "Like . . . the *best* kind of day."

"We'll have you out of there in a jiffy," said the third mouse, holding up a bent paper clip.

Chapter Three
Constance, Prudence, and Millicent

The mice used their paper clip to open the locks on each cage. A few minutes later, all the animals were set free in the gym.

"Welcome to Romeburg Elementary, the *best* school in the *world*," said one mouse. "I'm Constance, 5B."

"I'm Prudence, 3A," said the second mouse.

"And I'm Millicent. I was in 1C but now I'm in 1A, which is waaaay better because the teacher is nicer and I have a fabulous view."

"We *all* have a fabulous view, Millicent," said Constance.

"You live in the school?" asked Plum.

"Technically, we are classroom mice," said Constance.

"We're not classroom *pets*," said Prudence. "We are, like, studied and stuff."

"Mostly they just look at us and blow us kisses," said Millicent.

"We have to pretend to be caged during the day, but we totally escape after school," said Constance.

"That's why we kind of, like, rule the school," said Prudence.

"Except for the library," said Millicent. "That's ruled by the Professor."

"Professor?" said Itch, showing interest for the first time since being released.

"He's a turtle," said Prudence. "He's like a million years old or something. He's okay, but, you know, slow and old."

"Where is the library?" demanded Itch. "Tell me, mouse!"

"Jeez louise. Chill, little dude," said Constance. "What are you, anyway?"

"A ningbing who insists that you tell me where to find this library."

"Whatever. Second floor."

"Wait, Itch!" said Plum. "You can't just leave! We should stick together and wait for Lizzie to take us home tomorrow."

"Wait here if you want, Plum. Enjoy your little nest. I am going to explore the library and

attempt to have a conversation that is deeper than a knock-knock joke."

And with that, Itch strolled out of the gym and into the big unknown school.

"That little guy is soooo rude," said Millicent. "But he is right."

"You can't stay here all day," said Prudence.

"Borrrrring!" said Constance.

"I wouldn't mind having a look around," said Jeremy.

"Now listen, cat. We have rules around here. No trouble from you, got it?" said Millicent.

"Oh, sure," said Jeremy. "I wouldn't hurt any of you."

"Yeah, well, cats are cats."

"Jeremy is really nice," said Plum. "And he always stands by his word."

"If you say so," said Prudence. She turned her attention to Meg. "You are sooo pretty. Look at those feathers!"

"Thank you. My name is Meg," said Meg. "Plum here is even more colorful. You should see his plumage."

"Show us!" said Constance.

"Well," said Plum shyly.

"Now! Show us!" said Millicent.

"I don't . . . I don't want to right now," said Plum. He kept his tail feathers folded tight.

Constance let out a very dramatic sigh. She turned back to Meg.

"Are you shy and boring, too?"

"I don't think so," said Meg.

"You need to see the stage," said Prudence.

"Yes!" said Constance. "They're doing a real

play, with real lights, costumes, the whole thing."

"You would look so pretty onstage," said Prudence.

Meg blushed. "Wow. That does sound wonderful."

"Come on!" said Millicent.

"Okay," said Meg. "Plum? Kevin? Jeremy?

Myrna? Do you want to see the stage?"

"Just you, Meg," said Millicent. "It's, like, not big enough for everybody?"

"Your stage only fits three mice and one peacock?" asked Kevin. "That seems really small. I mean, I don't know anything about theater."

"Obviously," said Constance. "Meg? Coming?"

"I'll just go and have a peek. See you later, Plum?"

"Sure," said Plum. "Of course. Have fun."

Meg scurried off with the three giggling mice.

"I guess it's just us now," said Plum.

"Yep," said Jeremy. "Let's go exploring!"

"Oh. I thought we might just . . . stay here?" said Plum.

"No way," said Jeremy.

"Exploring might be fun," said Kevin. Kevin had his own Habitrail back at the zoo and was used to roaming about.

"Myrna?" asked Plum. "Are you going?"

Myrna was staring at the ceiling. She chirped, toddled back into her cage, closed her eyes, and fell asleep.

"Okay," said Plum, turning to the others. "Lead the way."

Plum followed Jeremy and Kevin out of the gym, but he did not share their excitement one bit.

Chapter Four
The Professor

Itch stood in the doorway of the school library.

"Ah," said Itch, taking a deep breath. "The smell of books."

He entered the library with hushed reverence. Here was Knowledge. Here were Facts. Science! History! (Also stories, but they were secondary to Facts.)

Itch would spend this otherwise disappointing snow day submerged in a sea of learning.

"Ningbing, I should think," rumbled a deep voice.

Across the library, an old turtle stood upon an open encyclopedia volume.

"Box turtle, I presume," said Itch with a slight bow.

"You are far from your ancestral homeland of . . . "

"Western Australia," said Itch.

"Capital?"

"Perth."

"Precisely," said the turtle. "Welcome to my library. I am the Professor."

Itch walked up to the turtle and glanced at the open encyclopedia.

"Volume X. Interesting choice," said Itch with a nod of approval.

"There are more words that begin with the letter X than the ordinary creature realizes," said the Professor.

"Why be an ordinary creature?" said Itch.

"Ah! A kindred spirit. Yes, young—"

"Itch."

"Yes, young Itch. I, too, have heard the clarion call to be *extraordinary*."

"Have you lived in this library long?" asked Itch.

"I have been here for many years, but my early education took place at the university," said the turtle.

He turned slowly to the wall behind him.

The wall was almost entirely made of windows. In the distance, high on a snow-covered hill, stood the grand campus of the university.

"Marvelous," said Itch. "What amazing thinking must go on there every day."

"Indeed," said the Professor. "And you? I take it you are part of the visiting zoo group. Have you been there long?"

"Yes," said Itch. "But I was recruited in Australia and spent many months with a very wise zoologist before arriving at the zoo."

Itch paused a moment. His eyes scanned the books, and beyond, the university on the hill.

"The Athensville Zoo is the finest zoo in the world, but . . . not all of the inhabitants share my thirst for knowledge."

"How so?" asked the Professor.

"Well, take the peacocks, for instance," said Itch. "They roam free, interacting with zoo visitors, and yet they squander that opportunity. Do they lecture the guests? No. Do they point out the educational signs and kiosks? Never. They flaunt their tails and pose for . . . *selfies*."

"A frivolous bird, the peacock," said the Professor. "Vain."

"Vain, foolish, silly, and utterly lacking any admirable qualities at all," said Itch.

"Well," said the turtle. "You are welcome to find comfort here in the library today. I daresay that I may prove to be more stimulating company."

Itch rubbed his little paws together. "Where shall we start?"

"Might I interest you in an exploration of my ancestors?" The Professor walked over to a nearby section of books.

"You mean . . . " said Itch, following eagerly.

"Dinosaurs!" exclaimed the Professor.

"Oh, joyous day!" squeaked Itch.

Chapter Five
Halls of Mystery and Danger

Jeremy and Kevin bounded down the hall happily, peering into classrooms, admiring the artwork hanging on the walls.

"Come on, Plum!" called Jeremy. "Put a little pep in your step!"

Plum peered down the long, dark hallway. Plum took a tiny step, but it had no pep whatsoever.

"Oooh, look at this, Plum!" said Kevin. "They have a water fountain just like at the zoo!"

Plum inched his way down the hall. This was nothing like the zoo, no matter how many water fountains it had. He knew every inch of the zoo. Plum knew his job; he knew the names of all the animals and zookeepers. He knew many of the loyal visitors. But this was school, and it was a complete mystery. Huge. Dark. Surrounded by ever-deepening snowdrifts. Plum wished he was home in the Great Tree watching the snow fall. At the zoo, the snow would be magical. Here at school, the snow was just one more hazard.

"Maybe we should go back to the gym," said Plum.

"What?" said Jeremy. "We've just started! There are three floors to explore. It'll be fun!"

"Well . . . "

"Are you okay, Plum?" asked Kevin.

"Uhhh . . . "

"We'll be fine," said Jeremy.

"You see," began Plum. "It's just that I'm . . . I'm a little—"

"Wowsers!" exclaimed Jeremy suddenly. "Art room!"

Jeremy and Kevin dashed into the art room, leaving Plum alone in the hall.

A light flickered.

Plum raced into the art room after his friends.

Kevin turned over a tin filled with pipe

cleaners and little fuzzy pom-poms, which he happily began to knock about with his snout.

"So soft!" Kevin said, giggling.

Jeremy stepped lightly on a long table in the middle of the room. Sheets of paper were laid on the table along with some pails of paint.

"Look!" said Jeremy. "If you step in the paint, you can leave paw prints on the paper."

"Let me try!" said Kevin.

"Don't you think you better not?" said Plum. "I mean, it isn't ours."

"Art is for everybody," said Jeremy seriously. "Lizzie said so."

"Look what I found," said Kevin. "Pointy scissors!"

"NO!" shouted Plum.

The others froze and stared at him.

"I am drawing the line at scissors," said Plum. "We'll get hurt!"

"No we won't," said Jeremy.

"We might!" said Plum. "Please, please, please, pretty please stop."

Jeremy exchanged a glance with Kevin. He hopped down to Plum.

"Plum," he said gently. "Are you scared?"

Plum looked at the little white cat. He looked

at the tiny giant elephant shrew.

"Yes," said Plum.

Kevin joined them. He put a paw on Plum's talon.

"It's okay, old buddy. We're here with you."

"I know," said Plum. "It's just . . . I'm sorry. I've never really felt *scared* before."

"You don't have to be sorry," said Jeremy. "Everyone gets scared. How about we go find Meg?"

Plum nodded. Finding Meg would be good. Then they could find Itch, and then everyone could go back to the cages, go to sleep, be rescued tomorrow, and return to the zoo.

"But first let's see the science classroom. They might have one of those exploding volcano models," said Kevin.

Plum's eyes widened to twice normal size.

Kevin sighed. "Ooookay. No volcanos. Sheesh."

Chapter Six
The Show Might Go On

"This is amazing!" said Meg in a hushed tone.

Meg stood in the center of the stage in the school auditorium. A backdrop had been painted to resemble an old-timey orphanage. Another backdrop was painted like the inside of a lavish mansion. There were wonderful props: buckets, brushes, and mops. Costumes were neatly hung to one side of the stage.

"And get ready for this," said Constance.

The mouse ran backstage. There was a click, and the stage was flooded with warm, colorful lights.

"Gee," said Meg, twirling around the stage.

"Here's the script," said Prudence.

"And some sheet music," said Millicent. "They play the background music on the CD player over there."

Meg examined the play script.

"It's about a poor orphan girl," she said.

"Yeah, but she doesn't *stay* poor," said Constance.

"That would be so boring," said Millicent.

"She's adopted by a super-rich guy and then, like, gets everything she wants ever," said Constance.

"How magical," said Meg. "Let's do a scene!"

"Now?" said Prudence.

"Sure," said Meg. "Here's one with a few different orphans. It has a song we can do, too."

Millicent switched the music on. The mice began to dance in the center of the stage. They were all doing different dances. Mostly they were just swishing their tails around and sticking their arms in the air.

They began to sing. Each sang a completely different song. And none of the songs went with the music that was playing.

"I think," said Meg, struggling to be heard over the noise, "I think you have the words a little wrong. Here are the lyrics."

"We know the song!" sang Constance.

"We know the whole play-ay-ay," trilled Prudence.

"Well, maybe we could all sing, you know, the same words?" asked Meg. "And practice for a while?"

"Practice?" said Millicent.

"But we're already awesome," said Constance.

"Let's do the scene from the beginning," said Meg. She pecked at the CD player and paused the music. "I think if we rehearse first, we'll be able to perform—"

The music clicked back on. Much louder. The mice jumped back into their various songs and dances. The lyrics mostly concerned really, really cool mice.

Meg turned the music off again.

"Let's do this right. Let's rehearse," said Meg. "Please?"

The mice froze in mid-dance. They stared at Meg.

"We. Don't. Need. To. Rehearse," said Constance.

"Because we rule the school," said Prudence.

"And we're awesome and cool and fun," said Millicent.

"We thought *you* were, too," said Constance.

The mice walked to the edge of the stage.

"But you're not, Meg. You're boring."

"Boring," repeated Prudence.

"Borrrring," said Millicent.

"Come on, mice," said Constance. "We have much cooler things to do."

The mice scurried away.

Meg stood alone on the stage. The lights were still on, the stage was still set. But she felt as if the curtain had fallen down right on top of her.

Chapter Seven
Lost and Found

Plum, Kevin, and Jeremy wandered down a dark third-floor hallway.

"We have definitely been down this hall before."

"No . . . this one is different," said Jeremy. "Isn't it?"

"Plum's right," said Kevin. "I recognize this water fountain."

Plum was feeling very anxious again. Where could the theater be? How big was Romeburg Elementary School? Should they have left a trail of bread crumbs or something? Where does one even *get* that many bread crumbs?

"I thought you had a good sense of direction, Kevin," said Jeremy.

"Me? Why would you think that?"

"You scoot all over the zoo in your Habitrail."

"But with the Habitrail, you only have two choices: forward or forward the other way," said Kevin.

"Does anyone remember how to get back to the gym?" asked Plum.

Silence.

"Great," said Plum.

"I'm pretty sure it was down," said Jeremy.

"There's a staircase at the end of the hall. Let's go down and look for either the theater or the gym."

"I guess that's a good plan," said Plum.

"What's the plan?" Kevin stuck his head out from yet another classroom.

"Stop going into classrooms!" said Plum.

"This one has a lot of paper snowflakes hanging from the ceiling," said Kevin.

"Haven't we had enough snow?" asked Plum. "Just follow the plan."

"Right," said Kevin. "Er, what is the plan?"

"DOWN!" said Plum and Jeremy.

"Okay! Okay!" said Kevin.

They headed to the staircase. At the top of the stairs, there was a small closet with an open door.

Plum and Jeremy started down the stairs. Kevin poked his head into the closet.

"Ooooh," he said. "Supplies!"

Kevin stepped inside. He admired the shelves of pencil boxes, crayons, and stacks of colored paper.

"This is really well organized. Hey, guys!"

Kevin looked back into the hall.

"Guys?"

Plum and Jeremy had descended two flights of stairs to the first floor. There was a sign pointing to the theater.

"Ta-da!" said Jeremy. "Nothing to fear, Plum."

They followed the sign down a very long hall, turned a corner, and found the entrance to the auditorium.

Meg sat on the stage, studying some sheet music.

"Meg!" called Plum.

Meg looked up. "Hi!"

"Wow! Look at all of this," said Jeremy, hopping up onstage.

"It will be a wonderful play. I wish I could see it," said Meg.

"Where are the mice?" asked Plum, joining them onstage.

Meg sighed.

"They didn't want to play. Not with me, anyway."

"Why?" asked Jeremy.

"I'm not cool," said Meg.

"Not cool?" said Plum. "Meg, you are the *coolest* of the cool. You are an iceberg of greatness. You're nice! You're smart! You're fun! You're the absolute best!"

"Thanks, Plum," said Meg. "Do you really think so?"

"I know so!" said Plum. "Just as I know every inch of the Athensville Zoo, I know that my friend Meg is the bee's knees!"

"And the cat's pajamas!" added Jeremy. "I should know."

"Aw," said Meg. "You guys are swell."

"So what have you been doing here since the mice left?" asked Jeremy.

"Learning this song," said Meg. "It really is beautiful. I'd love to hear the little girl perform it. Gosh, *I'd* love to perform it."

"Why don't you?" asked Plum.

"Yeah. We have a set and lights and everything," said Jeremy.

"I'll need to rehearse," said Meg.

"We can help," said Jeremy.

"And then we can be your audience," said Plum. "Me, Jeremy, and . . . "

Plum looked around. Jeremy looked around. Meg looked around.

" . . . Kevin."

"Oh, don't worry, Plum," said Jeremy. "He probably found the science room and is playing with a volcano. He'll be here soon."

Chapter Eight
The Phantom of the Furnace

Kevin descended the stairs repeating the words "down, down, down" as he went. Down one flight, down a second, past a sign pointing to the theater, and down one more long flight of stairs.

Kevin was in the school's basement. The dark, dusty, creepy basement. There were lots of mops, buckets, and broken desks. Spooky Halloween decorations filled one corner. Kevin looked away.

"Plum?" he called quietly. "Jeremy?"

Kevin walked deeper into the basement. The hallway ahead led either left or right.

"Too many choices!" said Kevin.

He stood for a few moments in the dark. Then he realized that if he turned his body one way or the other, well, then he would simply be going *forward*, not left or right. It would be almost like his Habitrail at the zoo.

So Kevin went forward. The basement became darker and darker. And then he hit a wall.

"Rats," said Kevin. "I guess it's the other forward direction."

Kevin turned and froze.

In the darkest of the very dark corners, two red eyes stared at him.

"Eep!" said Kevin.

The eyes kept staring.

"H-hello?" said Kevin. "I'm Kevin. From the zoo."

Stare.

"The Athensville Zoo?" said Kevin to clarify.

Stare.

"I don't mean to bother you," continued Kevin. "But . . . I'm kind of lost."

The red eyes blinked.

"Lost? Oh, I can help you!"

A red-eyed rat emerged from the shadows. The rat was rather dirty and scraggly looking.

"Thank you," said Kevin. "That's a relief."

"Not many people ever come down here," said the rat. "I try to stay out of sight. Sometimes I knock something over by accident, but when the janitor turns to look, I hide. He says, 'Must be the Phantom of the Furnace!' Because the furnace is over there."

"'Phantom of the Furnace' is a spooky name," said Kevin.

"Yeah," said the rat. "It even gives me the shivers."

"What is your real name?"

"Larry."

"That's a nice name."

"Thank you."

"So, Larry, can you help me get back to my friends?"

"Oh, sure," said Larry. "I know the school

pretty well. I used to live in a classroom."

"What happened?" asked Kevin.

"Well . . . some of the kids seemed to like me. But some would scream because I'm a rat. These three mice explained it to me one day. They let me out of my cage and told me it would be best if I never came back."

"What?" said Kevin. "That doesn't seem right."

"I am not cool, apparently."

"Probably because you live by the furnace," said Kevin.

"It would be better if I just led you part of the way and then told you where to go," said Larry.

"Nonsense," said Kevin. "You are helping me. You should meet my friends."

"Really?" said Larry.

"I insist!" said Kevin.

Larry licked his paw and straightened his fur a bit.

"Okay. But we have to wait until school is over."

"It's a snow day," said Kevin. "No one is here."

"Oh?" said Larry. "I don't have any windows down here. I thought it was a bit quiet. Let's go, then!"

Chapter Nine
Itch Goes to College

Itch stood in front of the library windows. It had been a fine day. He had read. He had discussed theories with the Professor. He had played Scrabble.

The day had provided the kind of intellectual nourishment that Itch had been craving for a long time. Itch remembered the zoologist who had recruited him for the zoo. They had spent many

days together. There had been private lectures,
books, and charts. At first learning had been a
challenge for the ningbing. But soon he began to
understand more and more. Soon Itch yearned to
learn *everything*.

He stared at the university on the distant hill.
So much knowledge. So close, yet so far.

"The grand university," said the Professor, who

had joined Itch at the window. "That, my friend, is where you belong. The department of zoological studies."

"It is impossible for me," said Itch.

"In theory," began the Professor, " . . . it is not *impossible*. In theory, that window can be opened. In theory, a ningbing who weighs only a few ounces could drop to the very soft, deep

snowdrifts below. In theory, that same light ningbing could run on top of the drifts without sinking. In theory, a ningbing could make it to the doors of the university."

The Professor cleared his throat. He sniffed.

"Of course, that's all just *theory*. Itch?"

Itch was no longer by the Professor's side.

Itch had opened the window.

Itch had jumped out the window.

And Itch had sunk deep into a snowdrift two flights below.

"Oh, dear!" said the Professor.

The turtle looked down at the tiny hole in the snowdrift where Itch had disappeared.

"My theory about the snowdrift seems to be incorrect!" the Professor called.

Itch, deep in the snow and thoroughly trapped, had already come to this same conclusion.

He scrambled with his little paws, but the snow simply crumbled around him. He could not climb out of the hole. More snow was falling. Soon he would be buried completely.

Itch was trapped.

Helpless.

Scared.

Chapter Ten
Turtle Run

"Do not despair, young Itch!" said the Professor.

The old turtle turned from the window. He must race like the wind to find help. He could do it. He thought of wise Aesop and his fable "The Tortoise and the Hare."

Slow and steady.

"Oh, drat," said the Professor. "Fast and steady, fast and steady!"

The Professor began to run as fast as his turtle legs would go.

Meanwhile, back in the theater, the performance was nearly ready. Plum was sitting in his seat in the auditorium. Jeremy was backstage with the lights. Meg was also backstage, preparing.

"Oooh!"

Plum turned to the back of the theater. Kevin and Larry had entered and stood admiring the set and lights.

"So magical!" said Kevin.

"Kevin! You found us!" Plum said with relief.

"My friend Larry helped me."

"Hi, Larry!" said Plum.

"I did get pretty lost," said Kevin. "I was in the basement."

Plum gulped.

"It was spooky, Plum."

Plum shook.

"Really, really spooky."

"Oh," said Plum in a small voice.

"But then I met Larry and everything worked out okey dokey!" said Kevin, beaming.

"Thank goodness," said Plum. "And you're just in time. Will you both please join me in the audience? The show is about to begin."

"Me?" said Larry.

"Of course," said Plum.

"*Larry?*" said Constance.

All turned once again. Constance, Millicent, and Prudence had returned. Next to them stood the Professor, trying to catch his breath.

"First, we find the Professor huffing and puffing in the halls looking for the zoo animals, and now we find the rat," said Millicent.

"What are *you* doing upstairs, Larry?" said Prudence.

Larry stood up a little straighter. "I was invited by my new friends. I am an audience member!"

"Audience for what?" asked Prudence.

"See for yourself!" said Plum. "We're ready, Jeremy!"

The lights in the theater dimmed. A single spotlight flicked on, revealing Meg standing center stage. The music switched on, and Meg began to sing.

She sang quietly at first, but with such heart and sincerity that everyone in the theater—Plum, Kevin, Larry, Jeremy, the mice, and the Professor—was instantly brought under her spell.

Meg sang about the sun coming out tomorrow. The song was sad and happy and hopeful all at the same time. It lifted the spirits of all who listened. Meg's voice grew loud and clear and beautiful. She ended with a big, inspiring high note.

Everyone erupted into applause.

Meg bowed.

"That. Was. Awesome!" said Constance.

"You really sang that perfectly!" said Millicent.

"I have, like, goose bumps!" said Prudence.

"Yes," said the Professor, who had finally caught his breath. "Well done indeed! What an extraordinary voice. It was enough to make one completely forget their—" The Professor's eyes widened. "Troubles."

"Are you okay?" asked Plum.

"I'm fine," said the Professor. "But I am not so sure about your friend Itch."

Chapter Eleven
Plum Takes the Plunge

Everyone hurried back to the library as fast as they could run.

"I'll catch up!" shouted the Professor.

The window was open, and a fierce wind was blowing snowflakes into the room.

Plum and Meg were the first to reach the window. Down below they could see the small hole where Itch was stuck.

"Oh, no!" said Meg. "He's so far . . . what can we—"

She didn't finish her question.

Plum had jumped out the window.

Chapter Twelve
A Call for Help

Plum landed with a soft *flumph* onto the lightly packed snow.

"Plum!" called Jeremy. "Are you okay?"

Plum sat up, sinking a little in the snow. "I'm fine!"

He began digging and soon found Itch shivering in his hole.

"Plum?" said Itch with amazement. "What . . . ?"

"Are you okay, Itch? I'm going to get you out of this."

"How?"

Plum looked up. The open window of the library was two very high stories up.

"Flying," said Plum.

"But you can't possibly fly that high," said Itch. "Peacocks can only leap a certain height."

"Well, I guess we'll have to try," said Plum. "Crawl onto my back."

Itch scrambled onto Plum's back. He held on.

"Here we go!" yelled Plum.

He flapped. He lifted a bit but fell back into the snow. He flapped harder. He lifted a bit more, but the wind and snow blew him back down to the drift.

Plum closed his eyes and flapped with every ounce of strength he had. Up they went. Up, up . . .

Down.

Plum panted in the snow.

"It's no use," said Itch.

"I just need to catch my breath," said Plum.

"I thought I could go to the university," said Itch. "I was foolish."

Plum shook the snow from his feathers. He eyed the distance to the window above.

"Plum . . . you didn't even hesitate," said Itch. "Without a plan or—"

"Well, I have a plan now," said Plum. "Keep trying until we make it. We're not giving up, Itch."

Itch nodded. He climbed back onto Plum.

Plum tried to fly, but now he was tired and the wind was stronger. They lifted, were tossed in the wind, and dropped back to the ground.

"It'll be okay, Itch."

Itch didn't say anything.

Back in the library, the other animals watched with growing panic.

"Oh, my!" said Kevin.

"They won't last long out there," said Constance.

"Definitely not," said Millicent.

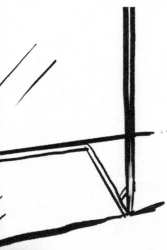

"Popsicles in an hour," said Prudence.

"Will you mice please be quiet!" said Meg. "You are not helping! We need to think!"

"I could jump out," said Jeremy.

"But then three of you would be stuck," said the Professor, joining the others. "We need to think of another way. We need to analyze the situation and come to the logical solution."

They all fell silent and thought hard about the logical solution.

At that moment Myrna the parrot toddled into the library. She looked at the books. She hopped to the window and gazed down at Plum and Itch.

Myrna waddled over to the librarian's station. Everyone watched her as she flapped up onto the neat desk. There was a calendar on the wall. The picture was of a white Persian cat lounging on a velvet chair surrounded by scones. At the bottom of the calendar were the words *Doily Gables Inn* and a phone number.

Myrna knocked the phone receiver from the cradle and pecked the phone number.

It rang. Someone answered on the other end. "Hello? Doily Gables. How may I help you?"

Myrna cleared her throat and then spoke in a crisp, clear voice. A crisp, clear *human* voice.

"Hello. It is urgent that I speak with Lizzie Rodriquez," said Myrna.

"Please hold."

Meg, Jeremy, and Kevin exchanged looks.

"Yes, Ms. Rodriquez," continued Myrna. "It appears that two of your animals have escaped and are trapped outside in the snow. Me? Just a concerned neighbor. Please do hurry."

Myrna pecked at the phone and hung up.

She turned to the others.

"Bloop!" she said.

Chapter Thirteen
Destiny

Lizzie and Principal Franklin arrived at the school minutes later. Plum and Itch were found, brought inside, and wrapped in warm, fuzzy blankets.

When they reached the gym, they discovered Meg, Jeremy, Kevin, and Myrna all locked safely in their traveling cages.

"Strange. I don't know how these two escaped.

I'm so sorry for the trouble, Principal Franklin,"
said Lizzie as she locked Plum and Itch back in
their cages.

"I'm just glad that the animals are unharmed.
Goodness! That window must have been left open
by accident. It sure was lucky a neighbor spotted
them!" said Principal Franklin.

"Chirrup!" said Myrna.

Lizzie knelt in front of Plum's cage.

"Plum, old friend," said Lizzie. "Don't go scaring me again, okay?"

"Sorry, Lizzie," said Plum. She nodded at his chirp.

Lizzie glanced over at Itch's cage.

"Same goes for you, Mr. Trouble Trousers."

Itch sighed.

"What have we here?" said Principal Franklin.

He reached down behind Kevin's cage. When he straightened back up, he was holding a scraggly, dirty rat.

"Larry?" said the principal with amazement.

"Who is this?" asked Lizzie.

"Oh," said the principal, holding Larry carefully so he could get a good look at him. "This is Larry. He was a classroom rat that went missing months ago. I was so worried."

"Really?" asked Larry.

"Oh, Larry. Come with me! I'll put a nice cage in my office for your new home. Safe and sound," said Principal Franklin. "The children will be

delighted to see you when they visit me."

"Some will probably still scream, though," Larry said to Kevin.

"I doubt that, my friend," said Kevin.

The principal carried Larry out the door. Lizzie took one more look back at the animals.

"I'll see you all tomorrow."

Lizzie turned out the lights and followed the principal down the hall.

The animals were tired. It had taken a while to warm up, but both Itch and Plum, snuggled in blankets and well-fed, were feeling much better.

"That was pretty awesome!"

Constance, Prudence, and Millicent entered the gym. "You zoo animals sure know how to make a scene! What do we do now?"

"I think we've had enough adventure for one day," said Meg.

Itch cleared his throat.

"Meg, perhaps you would indulge me. I know I've caused a lot of trouble today. Allow me to make it up to you," said Itch.

"What do you mean?" asked Kevin.

"Constance," said Itch. "If you would please unlock our cages once more."

The mice unlocked the cages.

"What's going on, Itch?" asked Plum.

"Please join me in the library in one hour," said Itch.

The animals agreed, and Itch exited the gym.

One hour later Plum, Meg, Jeremy, Kevin, Myrna, the mice, and Larry (who the mice released from his new home in the principal's office) entered the dimly lit library.

"Welcome," said the Professor. "Please have a seat on the rug over here."

The animals sat in rows as the Professor instructed. All were quiet and curious.

The SMART Board on the wall lit up. Itch stood on a podium beside it. He held a small remote control.

"Tonight, friends," Itch began, "I would like to present a very special lecture."

Itch clicked the remote and a photo of a peacock appeared on the screen.

"The peacock. The bravest animal I know," said Itch.

Plum sat up straight. Meg nudged him.

This was going to be a good lecture.

Chapter Fourteen
Home Again

The animals thoroughly enjoyed Itch's dynamic, fascinating lecture. Plum even learned a few facts that he hadn't known before.

After the lecture, they said good night and farewell to the animals of Romeburg Elementary School.

All slept well.

In the morning, the sun shone bright. The snow had stopped, and the roads were being cleared.

Lizzie arrived and loaded everyone into the zoo van. She waved to Principal Franklin and they started their slow, careful drive home.

The van pulled into the zoo hours later. Each animal was returned to its place: Itch to the

Small and Unusual Mammal Pavilion; Kevin to his Habitrail, where he was free to choose a pen to sleep in for the night; and Myrna to the Aviary. Lizzie carried Jeremy home to the apartment they shared.

Few visitors were at the zoo on this cold winter day. Plum and Meg were not required to mingle, guide, or delight. They strolled quietly to the Great Tree, where the rest of the peacock flock were nestled safely.

A light snow began to fall on the Athensville Zoo.

"Good to be home," said Meg.

"It sure is," said Plum.

"I heard Lizzie talking to the principal," said Meg. "They're planning another visit for the spring."

Plum nodded. He smiled.

He was looking forward to going to school again.

DRAW PLUM!

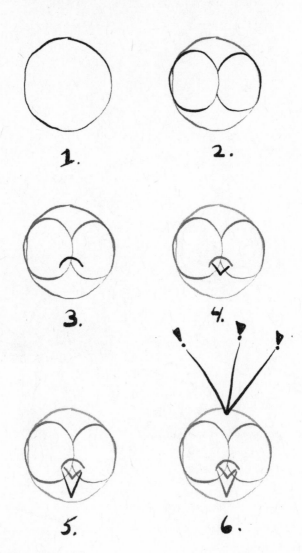

1.

2.

3.

4.

5.

6.